MW01078852

DADDY, CAN YOU MAKE ME TALL?

by Rona Milch Novick, PhD

Illustrated by Ana Sebastián

APPLES & HONEY PRESS

To Naomi, Nate, Yehuda, Amichai, Odelia, and Shlomo,
for filling my life with joy and giggles, and for
keeping me forever young! — RN

To those who read as much as they live. — AS

Apples & Honey Press
An Imprint of Behrman House Publishers
Millburn, New Jersey 07041
www.applesandhoneypress.com

ISBN 978-1-68115-597-5

Library of Congress Catalog Number: 2022031839

Design by Segal Creative
Art direction by Ann D. Koffsky
Printed in China

9 8 7 6 5 4 3 2 1

Shabbat is coming!

I can't reach my shirt.

Daddy, can you make me tall?

I can't make you tall,
but I can bring you a stool
and hold your hand
as you climb up and up and up
to the top step,
watching as you choose
the perfect shirt
and whisper, "I did it."

Mommy, can you find my comb?

I will help you look
and show you how to sort
your toys into the bins
and your caps onto the hooks.
And when you pick up the trucks you'll shout,
"I found my comb!"

And we'll help even your curls find their place.

Daddy, can you make the napkins fancy?

I will make a napkin sailboat
and show you how
to fold sailboats and swans,

and we will watch them float
past the shiny dishes and glasses
like a magical parade.

Mommy, can you fill my Kiddush cup?

I will fill it halfway and show you how to hold the bottle tight and tip it gently until your cup is filled with purple sweetness.

And *together* we will say the
blessing you learned,
and everyone will answer,
"Amen!"

Daddy, can you sing "Shabbat Shalom"?

I will sing the first line and help you sing the next.
Then we will sit in the light of the candles
as our dining room fills with music.

Daddy, Mommy, I'm big enough
to get ready for Shabbat!

Yes, you are! With a little help—

You chose your shirt,
and found your comb,
and made fancy napkins,
and filled your
Kiddush cup,
and sang
"Shabbat Shalom".

And now let's enjoy

this beautiful Shabbat we all made, together.

Our challenge as parents and caregivers of growing children is to find that balance between handholding and encouraging them to stretch and develop their skills. We may miss the lovely feeling of carrying our little ones in our arms. But the greatest gifts we can give our children are the skills to become independent and the confidence in their own abilities and growth.

Celebrating Shabbat can be the highlight of the week, with the opportunity for family sharing and togetherness. Making Shabbat a time of rest and enjoyment may require some preparation. In this book, the parents navigate the tension between their child's desire for independence and his age-limited skills by reaching a lovely compromise—they offer help—which supports their child's growing skill and success.

When we include our children as partners in our powerful traditions, we not only build their independence and confidence, but we gift them with a heritage rich and wonderful.

With warm wishes,

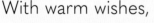